Ready, Set... Baby!

by Elizabeth Rusch

illustrated by Qin Leng

HOUGHTON MIFFLIN HARCOURT

Boston   New York

To my big kids, Cobi and Izzi. — E.R.

To Liam, for that babysitting day in Bordeaux. — Q.L.

www.hmhco.com

The text of this book is set in Humper Condense.
Library of Congress Cataloging-in-Publication Data is on file.
ISBN 978-0-544-47272-3

Manufactured in China
SCP 10 9 8 7 6 5 4 3 2 1
4500628501

A new baby's headed your way?

We got one of those!

Lots of people are probably telling you

what to expect, but kids in the know can

give you the real deal. Don't worry, it's

not as hard as it seems.

we were GREAT at it right away.

well, almost right away . . .

Anna and Oliver

THE BIG WAIT

When Mom and Dad told us we were going to have a new baby, they seemed excited for us, like it was our birthday or something. So we were excited too. Then a whole day passed, and another, and another . . . and there was *still* no baby in sight. We call this "The Big Wait."

Where's our baby?

WHOA!

"IN HERE" is where ice cream and bananas and yogurt go.

In here.

Moms have a special compartment inside for growing babies.

HOW THE BABY COMPARTMENT GROWS

3 months   6 months   9 months

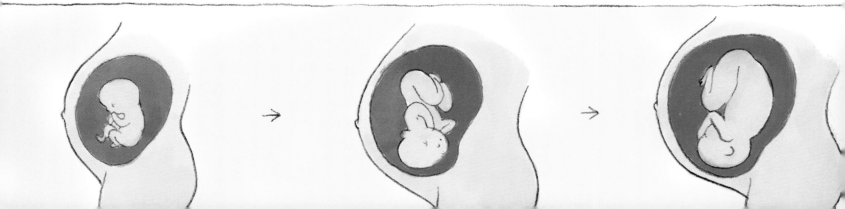

Mom's belly bulged like a balloon. We couldn't sit on her lap without sliding off. And she got a lot slower. She couldn't chase us around the park or wrestle anymore.

We had to find someone else to do that.

One day, Mom placed our palms on her tummy.

Day after day, we tapped **HELLO** on Mom's tummy. Some days our baby even tapped back.

YIKES!

She's kicking.

Our baby is kicking.

Kicking people is usually against the rules. But everyone makes exceptions for babies.

Then one morning . . .

THE BIG DAY!

While we waited for the baby to come, we built a fort,
dressed up our dragons, and swung on the swing 1,329 times.
And that was just the FIRST DAY.

Finally, we got to see our new baby. That's when the surprises really started.

MEET THE CONEHEAD

We had baby dolls, so we figured we knew what she would look like. **WRONG!**

Our baby had a conehead and red, wrinkly skin with little bumps all over her face.

Our baby's skin was warm and damp and squishy. Her hair felt softer than the fur on the softest teddy bear.

But she grips like an octopus. **YOWZA!**

Then our baby said something! She opened her mouth and . . .

SQUEAK

Now, Mom told us that our baby would not know how to talk and that she'd cry a lot. But she didn't tell us about all the *other* noises babies make.

GRUNT

SMACK

CHIRP

SNORT

Imagine walking past elephants, monkeys, and hippos in the zoo with your eyes closed. It's like that.

Babies' bottoms make some pretty funny noises too.

SPUTTER

Sounds like we need a new diaper, **STAT.**

GURGLE

SPLORT!

THE REAL SCOOP ON BABY POOP

We were NOT prepared for how many times a day our baby would need a diaper change.

We found out that it's like being the copilot, handing stuff like wipes, washcloths, and these funny T-shirts called onesies.

Don't worry, baby poop isn't too stinky. Not nearly as bad as dog poop. Sometimes it even smells milky or like buttery popcorn. And since babies are always bundled up like a blizzard is coming, it's your only chance to see the little trooper's tummy.

But get ready for a shocker.

Our baby had a little black stump. Yours will too. It's called the umbilical cord. It's where the baby was attached to Mom. Pretty soon, the stump will fall off and leave a perfect little belly button . . .

PLAYING— NOT!

After a diaper change, your baby may be ready for a nap.

THINGS NEW BABIES CAN'T DO

Sit up

Walk

Talk

THINGS NEW BABIES CAN DO

Fart

Pee and poop

Smile
(usually while farting)

Don't worry, it's not like you'll be lonely. Everybody we knew, and even people we didn't know, stopped by to meet the baby. But we have to warn you . . .

Our parents let us open some of the presents, but don't get your hopes up. There's nothing but . . .

WHAT TO DO WHILE EVERYONE STARES AT THE BABY

Sometimes we like to be part of the action. All you have to do is ask to hold your baby. It's cool.

Here's how it works. There's no way your parents are going to let you hold the baby standing up. So kick back and get comfy. Have an adult lay the baby on your lap.

Support the head! Support the head!

That means cradle the baby in the crook of your arm, like a football.

Football? I'm holding her head like a baseball!

The head will feel heavier than a football, though so rest your arm on a pillow.

We had a teeny bit of trouble the first time Oliver held our baby. He was so happy, he yelled . . .

We learned it works better to talk really, really softly—even whisper.

Babies can hear really well, kind of like dogs.

HI, BABY!

WAAAAAH!

Don't worry too much if your baby spits up on you.

Your baby isn't sick or anything. It's more like milk overflowing from a glass. **OOPS!**

GROSS!

It's easy to figure out how to fix this mess.

Change your shirt!

BABY DETECTIVE WORK

It can be harder to know how to handle it when your baby cries and cries.

This happens a lot in the late afternoon or early evening.

It's called "The Witching Hour."

All the adults have ideas about what to do, and you can come up with your own too.

Maybe she's cold.

Maybe she wants to see inside our fort.

I think she has gas.

URUURP!

BE ON THE LOOKOUT FOR THESE CLUES:

TIPS FOR ENTERTAINING

Actually, big kids are the absolute best at fixing a bored baby.

Start off easy, singing a song.

"Twinkle, twinkle, little star . . ."

If that doesn't work, launch into something more fun.

"On top of spaghetti . . ."

Don't forget to dance as silly as you can.

MORE TIPS FOR ENTERTAINING

Play peek-a-boo. | Make funny faces. | Make armpit farts. | Play peek-a-boo while making funny faces. | Play peek-a-boo while making funny faces and armpit farts.

If all this doesn't work, you might have a tired baby on your hands. We try to think about what we like when we're tired. Rub your baby's feet, or her back, or jiggle her crib like she's on a train ride.

Just don't get carried away and jiggle too hard or blow a whistle . . .

Mostly, it feels great to help with the new baby.
But it's not always easy. People always ask us . . .

That's okay. Your baby will be so happy to see you
when you're done.

And you'll be happy to
see your baby too.

Sometimes when we're with our new baby, time just flies by. But at the end of the day,
you may be in for one more surprise.

BIG KID BEDTIME ROUTINE

At first, our baby got to stay up later than we did!

No fair!

It's all that napping . . .

But eventually, your baby will have an earlier bedtime than you.

YES!

Then you can find your own special way to send your own special baby off to snoozeland . . .

MORE STUFF ABOUT LIFE WITH A NEW BABY

We hope you liked our book, but there are lots more places to learn about life with a new baby. Here are some of our favorites.

Websites

For more on what to expect when your mom is pregnant, how to adjust to a new baby, and even what to do if you don't get along with a brother or sister, visit kidshealth.org/kid/feeling/#cat20068.

Check out these cool drawings of what your new baby might look like growing inside your mom. www.babycentre.co.uk/pregnancy-week-by-week

Want to learn more about how your new baby's body—and yours—works? Look here: kidshealth.org/kid/htbw.

When you're old enough, you might be able to use these babysitting tips: kidshealth.org/teen/babysitting_center/tips_advice/babysit_olivia.html

Books

There's lots more information about how a baby grows inside a mom in the book: *What's in There?: All About Before You Were Born* by Robie H. Harris.

You can find answers to other questions you might have, such as "Why do new babies have to be held so much?" in *What to Expect When the New Baby Comes Home* by Heidi Murkoff.

It's fun to write notes or draw or take pictures of your new baby's first year. You can use a blank journal, or we also liked *The Big Sibling Book: Baby's First Year According to ME* by Amy Krouse Rosenthal.

TIPS FOR PARENTS ON LIFE WITH BIG KIDS AND NEW BABIES

We thought your parents might need some advice about the best way to handle all this stuff too. The author got ideas from experts (just like you got ideas from us!), so all these tips are . . .

BIG KID APPROVED!

Especially the part about presents and pancakes for dinner . . .

If your child is very young, consider waiting until the second half of your pregnancy to tell him or her about the new baby, if possible. Even three or four months can feel like an eternity.

Tell your child ahead of time who will care for him or her while you're having the baby.

Don't promise a new playmate. It will be a year or two until your children can truly play together.

Let your child pick out a small gift to welcome the baby, and pick up a few small gifts for the older child, especially from the new baby.

In the first few weeks, be prepared for your child to express anger or sadness. Help your child name his or her emotions and let your child know that all these feelings are normal.

Don't say: "You are going to love the new baby!" If your child doesn't love the baby right away, he or she may think there's something wrong inside.

Keep taking your child to playgroups or on playdates so he or she has a chance to socialize with friends.

Plan one-on-one time every day with the older child. Hire a babysitter or ask a family member or neighbor to hold your baby for an hour while you play with your older child.

Accept emotions while limiting behavior. If your child gets angry and tries to hit you or the baby, say: "I see you are angry, but you may not hit."

Maintain your child's regular mealtimes, bedtimes, and other routines. This will give your child a sense of security.

Be consistent with new rules. If your child must wash hands before touching the baby, make everyone wash hands before touching the baby. If you tell your child to be gentle with the baby, tell the baby to be gentle with him.

Say yes to reasonable requests, such as pancakes for dinner, when possible, to give your child a sense of control.

Say "I love you" as often as you can.